R0061644928

01/2012

W9-ABU-087

Dear Parent:

Congratulations! Your child is taking the first steps on an exciting journey. The destination? Independent reading!

STEP INTO READING® will help your child get there. The program offers five steps to reading success. Each step includes fun stories and colorful art. There are also Step into Reading Sticker Books, Step into Reading Math Readers, Step into Reading Phonics Readers, Step into Reading Write-In Readers, and Step into Reading Phonics Boxed Sets—a complete literacy program with something to interest every child.

Learning to Read, Step by Step!

Ready to Read   Preschool–Kindergarten
• big type and easy words • rhyme and rhythm • picture clues
For children who know the alphabet and are eager to begin reading.

Reading with Help   Preschool–Grade 1
• basic vocabulary • short sentences • simple stories
For children who recognize familiar words and sound out new words with help.

Reading on Your Own   Grades 1–3
• engaging characters • easy-to-follow plots • popular topics
For children who are ready to read on their own.

Reading Paragraphs   Grades 2–3
• challenging vocabulary • short paragraphs • exciting stories
For newly independent readers who read simple sentences with confidence.

Ready for Chapters   Grades 2–4
• chapters • longer paragraphs • full-color art
For children who want to take the plunge into chapter books but still like colorful pictures.

STEP INTO READING® is designed to give every child a successful reading experience. The grade levels are only guides. Children can progress through the steps at their own speed, developing confidence in their reading, no matter what their grade.

Remember, a lifetime love of reading starts with a single step!

For Ruby, Lucas,
and Theo
—J.L.W.

Step into Reading, Random House, and the Random House colophon are registered trademarks of Random House, Inc.

Visit us on the Web!
StepIntoReading.com
randomhouse.com/kids

Educators and librarians, for a variety of teaching tools, visit us at
randomhouse.com/teachers

ISBN 978-0-7364-2859-0 (trade) — ISBN 978-0-7364-8099-4 (lib. bdg.)

Printed in the United States of America   10 9 8 7 6 5 4 3 2 1

STEP INTO READING®

STEP 1

Happy Birthday, Princess!

By Jennifer Liberts Weinberg

Illustrated by Elisa Marrucchi

Random House 🏠 New York

Belle's birthday party
is so much fun!

Belle shares cake
with everyone.

Mix and stir.

Sew all day.

The birthday girl
is on her way!

Gifts for Tiana.

Lights that glow.

Cinderella's gifts have
lots of bows.

A sparkly ring.

A silver crown.

Rapunzel wears

a purple gown!

A wish come true!

Golden lights.

Birthday candles
shining bright!

Balloons
for Snow White.
Friends who care.

Jasmine has lots
of goodies to share!

Play a game.

Have some fun!

Cupcakes
for Ariel!
Yum, yum, yum!

Happy birthday,
Princess!